You Can't Have Too Many Friends!

MORDICAI GERSTEIN

Holiday House / New York

For my
wonderful daughter
Risa
who, like her father,
delights in
ducks
M. G.

This book is based on "Drakestail," a classic French fairy tale published by Charles Marelle in 1888
under the title *"Bout-d'-Canard"* in *Affenschwanz et Cetera*, a collection of popular stories.

Copyright © 2014 by Mordicai Gerstein
All Rights Reserved
HOLIDAY HOUSE is registered in the U.S. Patent and Trademark Office.
Printed and Bound in November 2013 at Toppan Leefung, DongGuan City, China.
The artwork was done on 2-ply Strathmore plate finish paper
with pen and ink, acrylic, and colored pencil.
www.holidayhouse.com
First Edition
1 3 5 7 9 10 8 6 4 2

Library of Congress Cataloging-in-Publication Data
Gerstein, Mordicai.
You can't have too many friends! / Mordicai Gerstein. — First edition.
pages cm
Summary: When jellybeans that Duck grew win a prize at the fair, the king comes and "borrows" some
but after much time passes Duck, accompanied by many of his friends, arrives at the castle to get them back.
ISBN 978-0-8234-2393-4 (hardcover)
[1. Friendship—Fiction. 2. Ducks—Fiction. 3. Kings, queens, rulers, etc.—Fiction.
4. Humorous stories.] I. Title. II. Title: You cannot have too many friends.
PZ7.G325You 2014
[E]—dc23
2013020997

Once
(maybe twice)
there was a duck named Duck.
He was small, but he worked hard.
He grew marshmallows, licorice whips,
and assorted jelly beans.
His jelly beans won first prize at the fair.

The king, hearing of Duck's jelly beans,
paid him a visit.

Off went the king with the jelly beans.

Duck takes but a few steps when he meets his friend Dog.

Dear Duck, where are you off to so jaunty and jolly?

To the king to get my jelly beans back.

Around the bend Duck meets his friend Babbling Brook, who burbles:

Quack, quack, quack!
Quack, quack, quack!
We're about to get my
jelly beans back!

In a second or two, the wasps
all crowd into Duck's ear.

That tickles!

Duck goes back around the house and bangs on the door again.

Quack, quack, quack! Quack, quack, quack! Please give my jelly beans back!

She leads him to the well, and he jumps in.

Duck happily scrambles up
her rungs, singing:

Quack, quack, quack!
Quack, quack, quack!
It's time to get my
jelly beans back!

The king's mother leads Duck
to the hot, hot oven.

Duck hops in, and she slams the door.

Goodness it's dark! And it's hot! I don't think my jelly beans are really here.

I'll cool things off and get you out.

It's Babbling Brook. She flows out of Duck's gullet, puts out the fire, and washes Duck out of the oven and right into the royal bathroom, where the king sits in his tub.

The king leaps out of his tub and down the stairs,
followed by his guards and his mother and the
wasps, who chase them all around the house.

Duck searches the house for his jelly beans.
But of course the king had eaten them.
All Duck can find are bags and boxes of
diamonds, emeralds, and rubies.

You can't eat these. Live and learn:
never loan jelly beans to a king.
I'll just grow some more.

And so Duck,
carrying his friends
as before,
starts for home.

Quack, quack, quack!
Quack, quack, quack!
I didn't get my
jelly beans back.

When they arrive, the king is there, waiting.

So they all had a delicious lunch of jelly beans,
and they are all still friends to this day.